BBC CHILDREN'S BOOKS
Published by the Penguin Group
Penguin Books Ltd, 80 Strand, London WC2R 0RL, England
Penguin Books Australia Ltd, 250 Camberwell Road,
Camberwell, Victoria 3124, Australia
First published by BBC Worldwide Ltd, 2003
Text and design © BBC Children's Books, 2003
This edition published by BBC Children's Books, 2005
CBeebies & logo™ BBC. © BBC 2002
10 9 8 7 6 5
Written by Iona Treahy
Based on the script by Diane Redmond
Based upon the television series
With thanks to HOT Animation
www.bobthebuilder.com
ISBN 1 405 90073 3
Printed in Italy

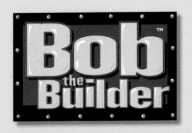

Bob's Egg and
Spoon Race

One sunny morning, the machines noticed that Bob and Wendy were acting strangely.

"Oh, er – why are Bob and Wendy running down the road balancing eggs on spoons?" asked Muck.

"Whooaaa!" shouted Roley. "Watch out!"

Crash!

"Are you OK, Bob?" Wendy asked, picking herself up.

"Fine, thanks," said Bob. "No bones broken, and look... no eggs broken either."

"Why didn't your eggs smash?" said Muck.

"Because they are hard-boiled," Bob explained. "We're using them to practise for the egg and spoon race. Mr Sabatini is making a giant pizza for the winner."

"That's enough practice, Bob. We'd better go and put in the doors at the Pizza Parlour, before the race," said Wendy.

Down at JJ's yard, JJ was also busy practising.

"Faster, faster, go Dad – go!" called Molly.

"You can make it," said Skip.

And JJ did make it – all the way to his office, where the telephone was ringing.

"Uh oh," said JJ, "back to work."

Over at Farmer Pickles's farm, Spud was complaining.

"All I ever do is carry eggs," he said, as he was given another tray of freshly-laid eggs.

"That's because everyone needs eggs to practise for the race," said Farmer Pickles.

"Yeah, well I'm going to win that race," said Spud, "because I want to eat that giant pizza."

"Hello," said Spud when he got to JJ's yard. "Farmer Pickles sent these eggs for JJ."

"Great!" said Trix. "More for me to practise with too."

Spud put an egg on Trix's prong. But when Trix tried to spin round with the egg, it fell on the ground and smashed!

"I just don't understand it," Trix said. "Before, the eggs sort of... bounced."

"What on earth's been going on here?" said JJ, as he and Molly came out of the office.

"Sorry," said Trix. "These eggs from Farmer Pickles keep breaking."

"That's because they are fresh eggs," explained JJ. "You were using hard-boiled eggs before."

Over at Mr Sabatini's pizza shop, Bob and Wendy were getting started on the doors.

"Can we fix it?" Bob called to the machines.

"Yes we can!" they called back.

First, Bob and Wendy put the spare bricks in a skip.

Then they fitted the new door frame.
Finally, Wendy put the glass in the frame,
using sticky putty.

No one saw Spud creep up and take
some putty.

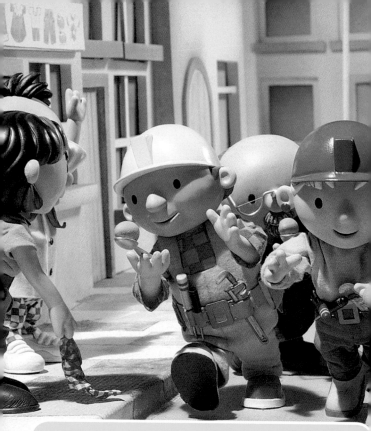

At last the shop was finished and it was
time for the egg and spoon race to begin.

Mrs Percival was waiting at the starting
line. She asked everyone to place their egg
on their spoon.

Then she called, "On your marks... get
set... GO!" and everyone sprinted off.

The tricky part was running at the same time as balancing the egg on the spoon.

JJ turned to Trix. "Remember, Trix – control!"

"I'll try, JJ!" said Trix, shaking completely out of control.

Spud wasn't in the lead
to begin with, but when
everyone else slowed
down for the bend in the
road, Spud kept up the
same speed.

"Look at me!" called
Spud. "Lah, lah, la-lah!"

Mrs Potts dropped her
egg as Spud ran past her.

Trix was really trying
her best, but she just
couldn't keep the egg on
her prong and keep up
with Spud.

"Yippeeee!" cried Spud, as he raced over the finishing line.

"Well done, Spud – that was amazing," praised Bob.

"Hurray!" called Muck and Dizzy.

"Yummy! I've won the giant pizza!" whooped Spud, swinging the spoon around. Strangely, the egg stayed on the spoon.

"Spud," said Bob. "How did you do that?"

Mrs Percival came running up. "Spud," she asked, "what's underneath your egg?"

Spud blushed. "Ooh! I used a bit of sticky stuff to stop my egg falling off."

"But that's cheating," said Mrs Percival.

"I'm really sorry, Mrs Percival," said Spud.

"Spud is out of the race," she announced.
"So... let me see... Trix is the winner!"

"Hurray!" called Muck and Dizzy again.
Spud looked sad.

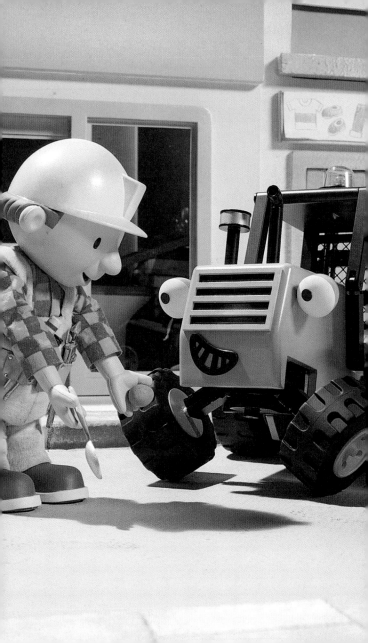

"Well done, Trix," said Bob. "All that practise paid off! And you kept control of your egg!"

Trix felt very proud.

Swish! The new double doors opened behind Bob and Trix...

...and there was Mr Sabatini with the giant pizza.

"Here she is!" he announced. "And bravo to the egg and spoon race winner – Trix!"

Trix moved towards the doors, lowered her prongs, picked up the pizza and smoothly backed up with it.

"There's a slice for everyone!" said Trix. "Tuck in."

Spud didn't think this included him, but when Trix gave him a wink, he raced forwards to grab the first slice.

"Oh, thanks, Trix!" said Spud.

"I see your egg still hasn't fallen off your spoon," joked Bob. Everyone laughed except Spud, who was too busy eating the wonderful pizza.

THE END.